First published 1990 by Walker Books Ltd
87 Vauxhall Walk, London SE11 5HJ

This edition published 2016

1 3 5 7 9 10 8 6 4 2

This book has been typeset in Plantin

Printed and bound in Germany by GGP

British Library Cataloguing in Publication Data:
a catalogue record for this book is available from
the British Library

ISBN 978-1-4063-7465-0

www.walker.co.uk

THE
SNOW LADY

A Tale of Trotter Street

WALKER BOOKS
AND SUBSIDIARIES
LONDON · BOSTON · SYDNEY · AUCKLAND

Sam's real name was Samantha but
everyone called her Sam. Sam's dog
was named Micawber but everyone
called him Mick. Sam and Mick
were very fond of each other.

In the mornings, when
Sam went to school
and Sam's mum and
dad and her big sister
Liz went to work,
Mick stayed at home `
to guard the house.

When school was
over Sam walked home
with her friend Barney
and his dad. As soon as
Mick heard Sam's footsteps he put
his front paws on the window-sill
and barked a joyful welcome. Sam

longed to put him on his lead right

away and run off up Trotter Street,

with Mick pulling her along and

sniffing excitedly at gates and lamp posts. But Mum was still at work and, as usual, she had arranged for Mrs Dean next door to keep an eye on Sam until everyone else came home.

Mrs Dean lived alone with her cat Fluff. Her house was very clean and tidy. The lace curtains were snowy white and the floor was polished like a skating rink. Mrs Dean welcomed Sam with a glass of milk and two plain biscuits. Sam balanced them on

her lap and tried not to drop
crumbs while she and Fluff
and Mrs Dean sat side by side
on Mrs Dean's beautiful blue
sofa and watched television.

Mick was never allowed into Mrs Dean's house. He and Fluff got on very badly whenever they met. Sam could hear him howling mournfully next door.

"Whatever has got into that dog?" said Mrs Dean.

She opened her front door and shushed at Mick from the doorstep, but he didn't take a bit of notice.

He just went on howling.

Sam and Mick were both glad when they heard mum's key in the lock.

Mrs Dean's garden was just as neat and tidy as her house. If

Mick got in there and started to

dig holes searching for imaginary

rabbits, or picked a fight with Fluff,

Mrs Dean became very cross.

Mrs Dean didn't even like Mick

to be in the street. Sam and Barney

and the other children often played
in Trotter Street after school and
Mick always joined in. But before
long Mrs Dean's face would appear
at her window. She would tap sharply

on the pane, then put her head
out and say to Sam: "That dog
really ought to be chained up. My
poor little Fluff is so frightened she
daren't come out." Or she would

say: "Would you mind asking your friends not to sit on my wall?" Or: "A little less noise, dear, please." And that was the end of their game.

But now the weather was getting too cold to play out of doors. One night the water from a leaking drain froze on the pavement outside Sam's

house, turning it into a sheet of ice. The Trotter Street children had a great time running up to it as fast as possible and seeing how far they could slide. They hung on to one another and all slid together in a chain. Wheee! It was just like the Winter Olympics! Mick ran

alongside, skidding and barking.

Soon Mrs Dean popped out wearing a shawl over her shoulders.

"That's very dangerous," she said. "You might easily break your arms or legs! Do stop at once."

Everyone stopped sliding except for Barney. He was at the end of the chain and just kept going. He cannoned into Harvey. Harvey cannoned into Billy, who fell against Mae, who slipped over, pulling Sam and the others with her. There was a terrific pile-up.

"I'm glad Mrs Dean doesn't live next door to us," Barney said later, when he and Sam were drying their feet. "She's always interfering and she hardly ever smiles. She's an old meanie. Mean Mrs Dean, I call her!"

It was getting near to Christmas.
People in Trotter Street were buying
Christmas trees and putting up
decorations. Mrs Dean hung a
wreath of plastic holly tied with
red ribbons on her door.

Everyone admired it except Mick, who took a savage dislike to it. He barked fiercely every time he caught sight of it. Sam had a terrible time trying to drag him past Mrs Dean's house whenever they went for a walk.

One day Mick got out on his own and worried the ribbon until he got one end of it between his teeth.

Then he pulled the whole thing down and ran off up Trotter Street with the wreath round his neck and the ribbons streaming out behind. Mrs Dean was very cross indeed.

After that, Mick was in bad disgrace.

Sam was pleased when she heard Mrs Dean telling Mum that she was planning to spend Christmas with her married son. And sure enough,

on the very day before Christmas
Eve, Sam saw her setting out in
a taxi, taking Fluff in a cat basket
and a great many parcels. Hurrah!
thought Sam.

Then something even better
happened. Out of a slate-grey sky
it began to snow. Big flakes whirled
down, covering the pavements
and parked cars of Trotter Street

with a soft, white blanket.

Next morning the sun came out
and so did Sam and Barney. They
decided to build a snowman where
the snow lay thickest, between

Sam's front gate
and Mrs Dean's.
First they piled the
snow into a big heap.
Mick watched with
interest

Soon there was
something which
looked like a person
with a round head,
stick arms and stones
for eyes, nose and
mouth.

"Let's give him a top hat and a
scarf and a pipe," said Barney, "then
he'll be a real snowman!"

Sam and Barney went indoors.

Mum was busy but she said they could pick out some old clothes from the top of the cupboard if they liked.

But Sam and Barney could not find any of the things they wanted, only a lot of hats and dresses

belonging to Mum and Liz.

"It'll just have to be a snow lady," Sam decided.

They dressed the snow lady in a hat and coat, put a shawl over her shoulders and hung a handbag on one of her stick arms. She looked very realistic.

"I know who she reminds me of," said Barney. And he moved the stones so that her mouth turned down instead of up.

He searched in the snow for some
more small stones and arranged
them where the snow lady's feet
would have been. The words stood
out clearly:

Sam giggled. The snow lady really
did look rather like Mrs Dean.
But Barney had not finished.
He rearranged the D in Dean to
make an M. Then the stones read:

Mrs Mean

"Lucky she's away,"
said Sam. "How awful
it would be if she could
see it!" Then they heard
Mum calling and ran
indoors taking Mick
with them.

The rest of the day was so busy
and exciting that Sam and Barney
forgot all about the snow lady.

Late that night, long after Barney
had wished them all a Happy
Christmas and gone home to hang

up his stocking, Sam was too excited to sleep. She got up, drew the curtains back a little and looked out at the street. Everything looked white and Christmassy, but big black clouds were scudding across the moon. When she caught sight of the snow lady, still standing there all alone, it gave her quite a shock.

Then Sam saw a taxi draw up. Out stepped Mrs Dean! The driver unloaded Fluff and the luggage and helped her into the house.

Mrs Dean walked right past the snow lady without even glancing at her.

But she'll see her tomorrow when it's light, thought Sam. It will hurt her feelings. And on Christmas Day too!

Sam decided she must go out at once and kick away the stones which spelled out the snow lady's name. She would

take the clothes off
too. It was *terribly
important!*

Sam crept quietly
downstairs and
began to put on
her coat over her pyjamas. But Mick
heard her and came running, barking
and making a great fuss.

Mum put her head around the
living room door. "Whatever are
you doing, Sam? You can't go out
at this time of night!" And she
packed Sam firmly off upstairs.

"The sooner you're asleep the sooner Christmas will be here," she said, kissing her good-night.

Still Sam could not get to sleep. She felt too awful about Mrs Dean. When she did fall asleep her dreams were full of excited visions of Mick, Fluff and the snow lady and lots of

Christmas parcels all tied up with
yards and yards of red ribbon. Mrs
Dean was inside one of the parcels.
She jumped out and then they were
all running and running… But it
was not feet Sam heard in her sleep.
It was rain.

When Sam woke up it was still
dark. Christmas morning! And yes,
the stocking at the foot of her bed
was full of exciting surprises. But
Sam did not put on her light yet.

Instead she ran to the window.
She could hardly see out because
rivulets of water were streaming

down the pane.
Below, in the street,
Sam could just
see the snow lady.
She seemed to
have slumped back
against the gate post and all around
her lay a puddle of water.

Then a great, warm hope leapt up
inside Sam. She skipped back into
bed and began to open her stocking.

As soon as Christmas Day had begun
properly and all the family had kissed
each other and given their presents,

Sam slipped out of the front door.

It had stopped raining. The snow lady had collapsed altogether. Her hat had fallen over her face and her clothes were limp and dripping.

She kicked the stones and scattered them about. Then she picked up the snow lady's clothes and pushed them into the dustbin.

She was only just in time. Mrs Dean's front door opened and out came Mrs

Dean, dressed for church.

Mum hurried to
their doorstep to
call out "Merry
Christmas, Mrs
Dean! I didn't
know you'd come back!"

"A Merry Christmas to you all,
Mrs Robinson. My son and his wife
have flu and couldn't have me to
stay after all," said Mrs Dean.

"Then of course you must come
and have Christmas dinner with us,"
Mum said at once.

"Why, thank you! That's very kind," said Mrs Dean. And her face melted.

Sam stood right in front of what was left of the snow lady. The name which had stood out so clearly in the snow was now just a jumble of stones lying in a pool of water. Sam shuffled them about with her feet, just in case.

"I expect you wish the snow had lasted longer," Mrs Dean said to Sam.

"Oh no, I don't mind a bit, really," said Sam. And she gave Mrs Dean one of her biggest most Christmassy smiles.

Shirley Hughes has illustrated more than 200 children's books and is one of the world's best-loved writers for children. She has won the Kate Greenaway Medal twice and has been awarded an OBE for her distinguished service to children's literature. In 2007, *Dogger* was voted the UK's favourite Kate Greenaway Medal-winning book of all time.

"No one can match Shirley Hughes in the simple mastery of both words and pictures."
Times Educational Supplement